Dear Parents:

Congratulations! Your child is taking the first steps on an exciting journey. The destination? Independent reading!

STEP INTO READING® will help your child get there. The program offers five steps to reading success. Each step includes fun stories and colorful art or photographs. In addition to original fiction and books with favorite characters, there are Step into Reading Non-Fiction Readers, Phonics Readers and Boxed Sets, Sticker Readers, and Comic Readers—a complete literacy program with something to interest every child.

Learning to Read, Step by Step!

Ready to Read   Preschool–Kindergarten
• big type and easy words • rhyme and rhythm • picture clues
For children who know the alphabet and are eager to begin reading.

Reading with Help   Preschool–Grade 1
• basic vocabulary • short sentences • simple stories
For children who recognize familiar words and sound out new words with help.

Reading on Your Own   Grades 1–3
• engaging characters • easy-to-follow plots • popular topics
For children who are ready to read on their own.

Reading Paragraphs   Grades 2–3
• challenging vocabulary • short paragraphs • exciting stories
For newly independent readers who read simple sentences with confidence.

Ready for Chapters   Grades 2–4
• chapters • longer paragraphs • full-color art
For children who want to take the plunge into chapter books but still like colorful pictures.

STEP INTO READING® is designed to give every child a successful reading experience. The grade levels are only guides; children will progress through the steps at their own speed, developing confidence in their reading.

Remember, a lifetime love of reading starts with a single step!

All rights reserved. Published in the United States by Random House Children's Books, a division of Penguin Random House LLC, New York.

Step into Reading, Random House, and the Random House colophon are registered trademarks of Penguin Random House LLC.

Visit us on the Web!
StepIntoReading.com
rhcbooks.com

Educators and librarians, for a variety of teaching tools, visit us at RHTeachersLibrarians.com

ISBN 978-0-593-30517-1 (trade) — ISBN 978-0-593-30518-8 (lib. bdg.)
ISBN 978-0-593-30519-5 (ebk)

Printed in the United States of America

10 9 8 7 6 5 4 3 2 1

Go, Dog. Go!

NETFLIX
A NETFLIX
ORIGINAL SERIES

Go, Team. Go!

by Tennant Redbank
illustrated by Alan Batson
Based on the Grand Sam script
written by Nicole Belisle

Random House 🏠 New York

Honk, honk, honk!
"Wake up, dogs!"
shouts Sam Whippet.

He is a race car driver.

Today is race day!

Which team will win?

Tag and Scooch?

Frank and Beans?

Gilber and

Cheddar Biscuit?

Sam tells them the rules
for the race.

Both dogs on a team
must reach the finish line
at the same time to win.
This race is about
teamwork!

"Go, dogs. Go!" Sam yells.

The Kibble Climb is first.
Tag and Frank race up
the hill made of dog food.
"You can't beat me!"
Tag tells Frank.

Wait!

Where are Tag's and

Frank's teammates?

Tag left Scooch behind.

Frank left Beans behind.

Gilber and Cheddar Biscuit
work as a team.
"We stick together!"
Gilber says.

Next, the teams
must cross
the Bone Bridges.
The bridges are bouncy!

Tag wants to win!

She forgets Scooch.

She runs.

Frank runs.

BOING!

"Oh no!" says Tag.

18

Scooch and Beans bounce
right off the bridges.
They fall into a ball pit!

Gilber and Cheddar Biscuit
take it slow.

"Slow is a go.
Fast is a no,"
says Cheddar Biscuit.
They are a good team.

The Yip Line is
the last part of the race.
It is very high.

"Don't look down,"
Tag tells Scooch.

Scooch looks down.

Oops!

He feels scared.

Tag zips off—without him!

Frank is right behind Tag.
But Beans is not
behind him!

Frank and Tag reach
the end of the race
at the same time.

"I won!" says Frank.

"I won!" says Tag.

27

Sam shakes his head.
Frank and Tag did not win.
"You did the work part,"
he says.

"But not the team part."
Gilber and Cheddar Biscuit
cross as a team.
They win!

Tag knows what to do.
She and Frank race back
to their buddies.

"Scooch, I'm sorry!"

Tag says.

"Up for a yip?"

Scooch grins.

One, two, three, four.

The dogs zip . . .

together.

Go, teams. Go!